CONTENTS

I

Incantation to the Stone God   3

Travelling Alone Is My Favourite Sickness   4

I Have Not Forgotten Some of My Strengths   5

On Waking   7

Highway Cottage   9

Incantation to the Stone God   11

II

The Outer Envelope of a Flower   15

The Poet's Dream   17

The River Rat   19

Operation Galileo   21

The Parishioner's Dream   23

A Singing Contest on Thorn Hill   25

Wych Elm Fields   26

Land Surveyance   29

The Prophecy of Old Bull   30

Hunter's Farm   32

Geraldine's Horselands   34

The Bride   36

In the Garden of Scarecrow Mannequins   38

III

Incantation to the Stone God   43

Crystal Lamp Auguries   44

After a Dream by the Banks of the River Frome   48

With My Mother at the Cattle Market Car Boot   54

On Visiting My Father's Grave   56

Way Back West   58

Down in Hemlock Wood   59

Incantation to the Stone God   63

Notes   65

Acknowledgements   67

Highway Cottage

ABOUT THE AUTHOR

Ralf Webb is the author of *Rotten Days in Late Summer*, which was shortlisted for the Forward Prize for Best First Collection, and the nonfiction book *Strange Relations*, which was shortlisted for the *Sunday Times* Young Writer of the Year Award. His poems, essays, and fiction have appeared widely, including in the *London Review of Books*, *Fantastic Man*, *Granta* and the *Guardian*. This is his second collection.

RALF WEBB

Highway Cottage

PENGUIN BOOKS

PENGUIN BOOKS

UK | USA | Canada | Ireland | Australia
India | New Zealand | South Africa

Penguin Books is part of the Penguin Random House group of companies
whose addresses can be found at global.penguinrandomhouse.com

Penguin Random House UK
One Embassy Gardens, 8 Viaduct Gardens, London SW11 7BW

penguin.co.uk

Penguin
Random House
UK

First published by Penguin Books 2025

001

Set in 10/13.75pt Warnock Pro
Typeset by Six Red Marbles UK, Thetford, Norfolk
Printed and bound in Great Britain by Clays Ltd, Elcograf S.p.A.

The authorized representative in the EEA is Penguin Random House Ireland,
Morrison Chambers, 32 Nassau Street, Dublin D02 YH68

A CIP catalogue record for this book is available from the British Library

ISBN: 978-1-802-06892-4

Penguin Random House is committed to a sustainable future
for our business, our readers and our planet. This book is made from
Forest Stewardship Council® certified paper.

Are you leaving for the country?
Do you feel like something's not real?

I

Incantation to the Stone God

Fingers of stone. Intestines of stone.
The eye and the eyelash of stone.
Incorruptible, blinding stone
That flashes every colour in the light.

When tears roll down my face
Salt streams down its face.
When I turn away from the world
It turns, and aches in place.

Teeth of stone. Genitals of stone.
Cuticles and stretch marks of stone.
Stalwart, unembarrassed stone
Spored with moss and lichen.

When my smile is taut and twisted
It bows its head and moans.
When I sweat and gag and vomit
It spews grit over the earth.

And when I, in disgust at myself, come
To its plinth with plans to destroy it –
When with my fists I pummel
Its stone flanks, thighs and buttocks –

I leave no marks. There is no change.
Only, as I fall at its feet to rest
It speaks to me in careful words
Of fortitude, mercy and great kindness.

Travelling Alone Is My Favourite Sickness

When I first arrived I thought I would buy a disposable camera.
In my Airbnb a week later the objects are in high definition.
A pair of leather boots, the lipstick I brought,
Empty cans of Diet Coke lined by the windowsill, scabbed over.
I am gorging on looks. I thought I'd do lots of things –
Like walks in parks – but have hardly left my room.

Anyway, why would I want pictures of the painful trees.
Accounts of my past lives in this city have dressed those trees in
        gauze.
(And a thumbprint in grease on the frame of a Suzuki.
And an expensive ticket to a Symbolist art gallery.
And cheap rosé, the grace of cheap rosé: all dressed in gauze.)
I want no photos. I make no telephone calls.

Anyway, what could I do with pictures of my painful outsides,
The dripping azaleas that hassle the boulevards.
The job of the picture is to account for love, to capture the
        simmering
Human glow. But that's probably impossible.
Atop the nightstand, my phone flashes with updates
On the mental health of all my friends. It would be vile not to
        answer.

The light in this room is my collaborator, a livid shade of red.
I begin to whirl a towel above my head, singing:
I had a good run! I have recorded this,
And replay it, so that the projection of myself
Is singing to me, *You had a good run.*
You ran well. You ruined. This is Projection Number One.

I Have Not Forgotten Some of My Strengths

I used to have a piece of string
Running from the top of my head
Down through my body,
Ending, wound, in the groin.
The string was pulled taut.
I danced! I was the life of the party.
Across the years, things stuck
To this string, and stayed there.
The string turned strut.
It held me up.
More than that, the strut became
The centre of myself,
Around which ideas orbited
As ribbons wind a maypole.
At the top, where it shot
From my skull, there was a light.
The light shone outward,
Washing over us all.
It wasn't a single event
That snapped the strut in two.
I think its fibres splintered
One by one, or rotted slowly away.
Now I walk around
With this broken thing, inside,
And the light shudders:
It might, at times, illuminate the face
Of someone vaguely familiar,
Their teeth slapped on a windscreen
Wet with rain, and racing
Through the night into nothing.
When I meet old friends

In the park, and they laugh,
So animated with their gestures
They spill coffee over themselves –
I wonder what I've done wrong.
I don't want to ruin your afternoon –
I have so many nice things to say –
But the words won't come out.
So I dig my fingertips
Into their shoulders,
And cling to that flesh.
It is a wonderful place to grip the body.
Touching them, there is a warm
Pinkish glow, and something
Quickens the blood.
Our eyes are huge and dewy, like a cow's.
We slouch through city parks
With dirt under our nails,
Ears packed full of wax,
Mouths dripping, lush as carnations.

On Waking

Very late one night
I walked down to the boiler room
Inside my head.
I was having a violent nightmare
About my mother.
Except it wasn't my mother.
It was an impostor.
Down in the dark boiler room
In the block of flats
Inside my head, the air
Is thick and close.
As though it is not air at all
But a spore cloud
Trying to enter the body
Through its permeable layers.
In the boiler room
At the bottom of the block of flats
Where I live inside my head
Stood my not-mother,
Peering out from behind
A column of concrete.
She was both visible and invisible.
As obvious as a petrified tree,
And yet absent:
The negation of light.
I wanted to run,
But my legs weren't there.
I wanted to scream,
But syrup clogged my mouth.
The boiler room began to hum.
Its pipes began to ache and hiss

As my not-mother
Made her approach.
Then, a knife. And I woke.
Scrabbling at my belly,
Searching for wounds.
Later, at the window,
Gnawing half a cigarette,
Letting the bitter night
Wash away my sweat,
I found no relief.
A fact of injury, on waking,
Would have been better
Than these endless ellipses
Which are placed
Around all our necks
At birth, by love
And the terror that lives inside that love.
I am supposed to pick up the phone.
I am supposed to call and say,
Tell me about your life.
Start from the very beginning.

Highway Cottage

There is a little house, down a little lane,
Somewhere way out west
Between one place and another place.
It is a place of rest.
The house is very charming and casual
And all the people who stay in it
Are charming and casual, too.
Out on the veranda
There's an ancient wooden table.
It looks made for a banquet.
Sturdy enough to use as a raft,
In case of flood. Handsome enough for a coffin.

I think I stayed there, once. A guest brought out
A hefty jug of wine, and said,
Let's play cards all night.
The dealer was throwing figs at eternity.
My anxieties went scurrying away,
Like mice into the larder.
And my fears vanished, one by one:
The dread of being alone,
And the despotism of indecision.
Nevertheless, I remained aware
(As one is aware of a stone in the shoe)
Of the abandoned quarry, not far down the lane.

There was a mysterious *splosh* and *splash*
In the quarry's lake, throughout the night.
Probably kids chucking rocks
From the bank. Or the earth
Talking to itself in its sleep.

Or somebody dumping evidence
Where the lake runs deep . . .
As the Buck Moon was kicking the sun
Out of bed, I swam off the wine
In that fabulously cool, green water.
I was happy-sad, if not happy-happy. So happy,
I could've sunk, and it wouldn't have mattered.

Incantation to the Stone God

In a dream, as a toddler, I was put
On a coach and driven alone
To a museum on a promontory.

The entire building was empty.
There were no artefacts on display,
Nor any other visitors. My palms

Echoed among colonnades
As I crawled the marble corridors.
Then, in the dim coral light

At the end of a long hall,
I saw it: a single statue
Of a figure with a spherical head.

I crawled past, and looked back.
The figure was still. I continued
Into the darkness, until I heard

The hideous rapture of stone splitting
From stone, as the figure detached
Its mottled limbs from the plinth

And tumbled to the mirrored floor.
It began to carry its heavy carcass
Towards me, like me, on all fours.

Round and round the museum I went
With the figure following behind.
When I thought I'd moved far away

I looked over my shoulder to see
That marionette of granite halted,
Swivelling its head in mimicry.

II

The Outer Envelope of a Flower

I'm driving along the ridge of the unlit valley at night
With the two sisters in furs.
What has happened to us these past years?
Not much, to be honest. We are young for ever.
The Spotify remains the same:
Teenage music from our parents' teenage years.
It's the same kind of story,
That seems to come down from long ago . . .
The valley at night: a vast, soft, oozing stone.
It leaks ambrosia from its pores,
Which is sustaining in perpetuity,
Provided we stay away from it. More or less permanently.

Ninety miles per hour past the ice-cream farm.
It's true – I still like to cruise annihilation.
We have had some ales. Our speech is blurred.
Let me adjust . . . I'd just like to . . . Let the wheel drift
And roll free, getting intimate with the earth.
If I could lay my head down, if I could lay my head down
In a dell on the moonlit clover!
A little lamb aglow on the sign of an inn
Beamed by the hybrid Toyota Corolla.
It is the season: over the hills and through the woods
The head-to-back stun-kill, shackle, hoist and blood.

Somewhere around here, in a postwar ex-council house
My stepdad will be falling asleep
In front of localised cremation ads.
What dreams of your own are you siloing away
In the folds of those vintage ermine coats?
An international career, an extremely pleasant salary,

A busy life split between the cafe-desolation
Of Athens, Paris, Berlin and Rome,
And the putrid leaf mould of this green-gold valley . . .

We did, after all, live by fields a long time
And have been cold a long time,
Waking year after year to nothing
But the promised perfection of an early marriage,
Screaming kiddies, frozen foods.
So why shouldn't we take a swipe at the world?
Or bid, concertedly, for everything?
The descent. Hairpins. Blind curves.

Did you ever hear that folk tale about a local woman
Who drowned herself down there
To escape the violence of the man
She was wedded to?
Her hair became the reeds.
The reeds by the water.
No, wait, it didn't go like that.
I don't remember it at all, actually.

The Poet's Dream

On the verge of red rocks
At the edge of the gulley
That goes down to the stream, I stood.
I saw him pass, smile and beckon.
He bade me leave the stones,
But I moved not. O my soul.

The ivy and white wood anemones
Upon the verge of red rocks . . .
Two sulphur butterflies,
The perfume of poplar sheathes,
Love-in-idleness, love-in-a-mist,
Love-lies-bleeding. O my soul.

He bade me leave the stones.
I moved not. I felt myself
Half-consciously upon the point
Of translating my dreams
About love into fact.
It bloomed up, like a spontaneous flower

From the conditions of our intercourse
As comrades. Like a peculiar plant
That has its roots in something real . . .
Devil-in-the-bush, hollyhocks,
Carnations: the fairyland of boyhood.
The final expression of mutual love.

The nature of art is to live out a dream.
But I was made to lock
The dream in a black tin box
And hide the box away.
The key was cast into the river,
From the verge of red rocks.

The River Rat

The water knows what the darkness knows. The only truth
Is how to travel from this side
To the other. I try to explain it to my friends:
Memories are turned to ash and scattered
At least monthly by our neighbours, here.
They told me to shut up. Anointed me the river rat.

These boys, my friends, don't even know the names
Of the river's tributaries and arteries. Certainly not its source.
They've a mistaken impression in the mind's eye
Of a mountain, or its opposite.
Snow and snowmen at the pyramid point,
Snow-limbs in white fire melting into freshwater.

In summer we all come here, where brook meets river.
Upon its banks we get undressed,
Compare the lumps and mounds and burgeoning tufts
Of darkish hair upon our bodies
And prod them, before slipping
Like cat's tongues in and out of the shallows.

These boys, my friends, have immaculate metabolisms.
The sons of farmers and former football legends
Now all pretty with gin blossoms.
Flush with pig fat and cider, they face-plant the river
And never get cold. I sit and tremble
On a tree root, in sunlight the colour of ashtray water,

Fearful of rats' piss, rats' shit, *what if I swallowed it . . . ?*
My friends, meanwhile, mock drown each other.
A game they learned called water torture.
Bubbles and black slime down in the dark crescent.
Then, their red guppy mouths suckling on air
In a lush, bright action of terror and baptisement.

Operation Galileo

'Here are creatures who are even afraid of us' — Hare

A drone unit encamped on Hay Lane,
Sent to track and capture
Men suspected of animal torture:
Hare coursers on the downs
In an heirloom jeep, with English greyhounds.

Freedom is flight without leaving the earth.
The drone pilot gnaws at his callouses,
Presses both thumbs
Onto the joysticks, and hums
Wagner to his boys. Valkyries aren't killers;

They're bureaucrats, employed
To select and convey the already dead.
To command one is celestial.
The quadcopter ('built to empower,
Destined to serve') lifts above the oak heads.

Jackknifing the drone over the downs at dawn
Feels, to the pilot, like fucking:
Manipulation of a complex system,
So much procedural pushing and prodding
Until he generates a satisfactory reaction.

The drone is a metal fistful of mosquitoes.
Its needling, whining thrum
Fills the pursued men with adrenaline.
Fear is its own conquest:
Inciting it in another terminates one's own.

The pilot's been told the men are barbarians.
A menace and a blight
On a law-abiding rural community.
But he thinks of them, instead,
As pudgy vessels of pulsating light,

Red-and-green amoebas squirming
In the drone's thermal cameras.
He thinks his eye a god's eye,
His power total, primed to pin
Their lives to history, with a button's push.

The Parishioner's Dream

The brook's cut gorges and grooves into memory.
Underground, the skeletons of ancient metalworkers
Carry in their marrow thin dreams of fertility.
Skulls caved in, by bone and flint.
Bloodlust is an end, evergreen, in itself.
We come to lay gas pipes and discover them.

We come to lay waste to the Gypsies of the river
In parish council meetings, with lots of hand-wringing:
I for one don't want their shit (minute-taker
Delete expletive) expelled in our water.
Would I were a reaper I'd seek them in the corn.
Would I were a keeper I'd hunt them with my horn.

We come to conduct health surveys. Later, police raids.
In a dream, I fathered, or fostered,
A bushel of three apple-bright daughters.
They'd many different mothers. Good local women.
The pink daughters and their ripe mothers
Glided by and guarded the water, hand in hand . . .

Dear councilmen, to preserve our countryside,
We need to support the businesses
And property owners who manage the land.
Caretaking of the Earth.
It really is God's work, or the work of a god –
See our sacred river in beautiful fucking spring

Flowing past the first-rate shooting gurus
At Egypt Lodge, teaching on the corporate package.
What better way to keep tradition alive
Than an afternoon of simulated game?
The Wagyu Beef Connoisseur Cigar Shoot.
Rifle butts jammed into shoulders. Cocked.

A Singing Contest on Thorn Hill

Tell me of the different ways
To carve the heart out of the country;
To do this without drawing blood,
And without getting bloody.

You mustn't write, you mustn't sing:
There's no poetry in bureaucracy.
Turn the hourglass, let it run,
And scorch the earth through apathy.

Reveal to me the special schemes
That render indolence so powerful,
Make sloth a perfect instrument
And time a perfect scalpel.

For ten long years ignore the pleas
Of those who live in Wych Elm Fields.
Let ten years' damp, and rain, and rust
Supply, through ruin, a sunny yield.

There is poetry in these plans
Just as our sewage runs through sod:
For it takes craft to summon ruin,
And gather rain into a flood.

Wych Elm Fields

Wrecked lime kilns and red-brick eel houses
Near the heart of the heart of the country;
Abraded outlines of draft societies
Or a humdrum bucolic in the attic of memory.
In a black hanger, men make cable for military vehicles,
Place bets on the cost of petrol at Murco.

Wych Elm Fields. Council-run. Fifty pitches
Lie along an asphalt curve, opposite
The maize maze. Separated by chain-link
From the Laser Clinic car park, abutting the mortuary,
Where kids from town kill time, skip rope,
Improvise seances in a borrowed Prius.

A certain kind of light deciphers whatever it sees.
Green rays once leached through tangled pillars
To describe the lives of Wych Elm Fields.
The trees were cleared. Now the moon,
When it rises, makes flat lanterns of the puddles
Ricocheting reflections in the warp of dreams.

Evelyn at the kitchen sink, humming hymns.
In bad weather, she thinks of Chaplain Johnson,
His drip-drop declarations of ordinary love
Housed in the gaps between spoken words.
And a childhood memory of little brown violins
Overheard in a deluge in a market.

Water music. Sewage, blockage, loony rain.
Evelyn's home has been made the basin
Of an arbitrary floodplain. Feels semitropic,

In summer, bindweed flowers like thousands
Of tiny dish antennae. 'Environmental Protection'
Is a misnomer. Phone them and it just rings. And rings.

*

Evelyn charges the county with neglect. On Thorn Hill,
In the Guildhall, councillors sit under oils
Of kings. They make portals of dust
With their mouths when they yawn,
Risk-assessing proposals from private bidders.
Men who want to buy Wych Elm, and ease their pain.

Men embodied by confirmation statements
And profit models. Men who conjure promises
Of creative solutions, targets and progress
Under gypsum board and fluorescent tubes,
In rooms that exist in a reality anterior to weather,
Lighted the colour of lack, the colour of absence.

Evelyn eyes the moonlit asphalt. A mirror that purls.
The place where her daughter, as a toddler,
Drew mountains and oceans, stick figures
Floating in bubble hearts. A new country, made of chalk.
She still steps over the cracks when she visits.
The cracks in the asphalt. Where she learned to walk.

What was it the Chaplain said? Love is a hornet
Between the eyes. Home is a water lily
Blooming in the mouth. Both demand recognition.
Evelyn paints blue skies over the day room's

Soured walls. Yes, she thinks. Love
Is an angry god; and home an act of imagination.

Evelyn's wind chimes flacker in an angelic storm.
Two decades of vivid harmonies, that grow
More spectacular each passing year. This makes
A life: an accretion of echoes, gambolling
Through water meadows. Echoes and truths.
Progress is a heavy wheel. One that never moves.

Land Surveyance

It's quick to kill anything that takes a long time to grow.
A man in a boiler suit lumbers over the parched meadow.
He touches with cracked hands gold follicles of grass tips,
A million pristine anemones topped with all-seeing filament,
Runs his fingers through these hairy antennae. Sweat sticks
Cotton to armpits. He imagines a fraternity of men like him
Inculcated in geodesy, alliances lubricated by scale and colloquy:
We dream of deserts. We dream of oceans. We dream of Mars.
Little morning stars of teasel vibrate in his peripherals.
And the goldfinches, what are they saying? It is a language
Unlike any other, echoing beneath the ceilings of half-starved trees.
The language seems to travel on light, chaotically scribed:
A cassette tape rewound and unspooling. It makes him feel,
Suddenly, discontent with his stolidity, vaguely aware
Of a melting sensation in the toe of his shoe, perturbed
By a jewel of magnesium flaring in his skull, between his eyes,
Sending rods of white heat pulsing across his scalp,
Running down the back of his neck. His crotch stings.
Bugs clamp mouthparts into patches of flesh on his ankles
And the milk-white swatch of skin in the crook of his elbow
Where a vein throbs like a slow-moving worm. It burns.
The crotch. Ink in the ballpoint clipped to his breast pocket
Congeals like bad blue blood, clumps to the inner cylinder.
And the goldfinches, what are they saying? It is a language
Utterly unlike his own, which rivets the objects in the world
To the world, binds his body to the earth and the earth to his body:
I'm the light that can't be seen, I'm the surplus polythene,
I am the skeleton on the green, and through my sight flow
Significant renderings of insignificant empires.
It takes a long time to grow anything worth growing.

The Prophecy of Old Bull

The river wends, then pools, uncoils and distends,
Rushes against stones, mimicking sounds.
The sound of starlight dripping out of the black,
The sound of a radio broadcasting riddles
Or stirrups sniffling along a ragged road,
This plodding of brook on rock and aluminium.

This is the pissing place of Old Bull, in leather,
Pissing away two litres of his favourite beer-water –
Old Bull in blue Levis and peacock feathers.
A bird-god military plane boulders overhead.
In Bull's eye, the holy paranoid nuclear war
Is on its way to green green land. It's real, this time.

Old Bull: half a mechanical man, filled with alloys.
Fused back together in the aftermath
Of a Kawasaki bike crash, on Thorn Hill,
When he was only a boy of seventeen.
I've a plate in my skull, he says. Feel me, here.
Feel how it's cold. All my insides, colder than stone.

Old Bull envisions a rapture. The frail like him
Will be left down here on Earth to starve
In dusts and dirts, in radioactive wastes
While the young set off among the stars
To toss or spit or sell our crap
Across the whole mother-fucking universe.

Only initiates like Bull are trained to hear
The secrets cast off in whispers
From the pissing-place, the swollen brook,
Its silt gums speared with broken bottles.
We used to wear pins in our ears, hears Bull.
And now they're putting chips in our heads.

Hunter's Farm

Feeling the weight of the thirteenth hound
(Bullet-brained, medulla expunged)
Loosen from my hands;
Hearing it hit the dustbin's metal innards:
It's a relief like clearing catarrh
From the throat, or taking a shit
On a cold winter's morning.
A dozen and one dogs killed
For old age and complacency.
I loved every one. In my own way.
But dead weight's dead weight,
And dying's better than living aimlessly.

All animals, and men, have purpose.
Mine is to dispose of and house
The exhausted. Unmarked bins
Overflowing with the heads
Of calves and horses, bollocks
And entrails. I let the healthy dogs
Eat what they please, spread feed
For the white chickens
Across the bloodstained concrete.
Vermin glean whatever's left.
Biosecurity, in practice, is flexible.
And one person's neglect is another's efficiency.

As I pressed the muzzle to her head . . .
The way she looked up at me,
So much loyalty and obedience.
Eyes like moons, like my wife's.
I keep the long-barrelled Humane Killer

In the gun cabinet, beside the bed
Where we sleep. It's our way of life.
All that we love of the countryside.
You might call me evil; I call that charge
An imperfect understanding of the world.
Evil lives, to be sure. It lives in ignorance,
And I am nothing if not an enlightened man.

Geraldine's Horselands

In the conservatory where the moss has grown
Into green phosphorescent curtains
Along the windowpane, retired Geraldine
Reclines on the chaise longue,
Rocking ice against crystal, spilling gin
Over the silk chrysanthemums of her kimono.

Geraldine's neck clicks westward. She peers
Past her reflection, out into the inherited estate,
To the petrified tree by the river's edge,
A watchman guarding her from
The equine ghosts that she imagines
Roam the banks, speaking in men's tongues.

The indigo fields undulate.
Nights like this, when hope seems as thin
As a yellow ribbon, Geraldine remembers
The terrifying candlelight of her girlhood:
Musty rays in the stables, like prison bars,
Pin-striping the backs of her father's horses.

There was a bay mare named Wilderness
To whom she told secrets, galloping past
Old flock mills on riverside bridle paths
And the frothy steps of tumbling weirs.
Wilderness was an endless answer to a question
She couldn't articulate. Until the water hemlock.

When her father shot the horse, it didn't sound
A thing like she had imagined. Not expulsion,
But suction, as though he'd siphoned
All her secrets from its skull. Thereafter, Geraldine
Saw her life as a series of blue implosions;
A manor house caving in under the strain of English ivy.

The Bride

To begin at the beginning would take too long
(Rapid evaporation, eruptions, storms)
But the locale contains both beginning and end:
Boot prints on baggies and frustrated condoms
On the sludge banks of Bull's Brook,
Down a back alley behind the Best Western.

A little way upriver, a wedding reception
At the Sheep Hide Inn ('A Place to Hide In!').
The grapevine meshed to the trellis
Evokes Christendom and eternity.
Bluebottles shocked in the EasyZap
Sputter and fall like prosody.

The groom walked out of the woods, one day,
And into the bride's life. As if by accident.
His hands big enough to captain and steer
The stories of whomever he wishes to acquire.
Now, all at once, he grins and shunts
A tankard against her father's, while she watches.

There's a river flower pinned to his lapel.
He invented a name for it: mud-sprite,
Sweet blossom of the sewage pipes.
After the ceremonies, he takes her arm.
Follow me, my one true love, to the riverside:
On a bed of bulrushes, I'll make of you a bride.

In the valley, a creaking kissing gate agitates
Memories from several centuries: a spate
Of song no man could tame, nor rationalize.
I will come, my love, and learn the names
You have given to the flowers. Then, I will create
New names. Ones he will never recognise.

In the Garden of Scarecrow Mannequins

All our dreams are different. The pinkish dusk
And late maize, in amber hues,
Have softened my edges.
The conversation is getting confused.
Alice and Jack with two little tykes
And careers in human resources.
The tykes dig up toy dinosaurs
From desiccated earth. Infinity is a mortgage.

I have come back here to reclaim our dreams
Like a knight in an old legend.
But, having arrived, I find I'm not needed.
I even seem foolish. Ill-omened.
What was it, anyway, that we once wanted?
To own a house and land, silver and gold?
We stuck 'FOR SALE' signs in our dreams.
Because we are canny, our dreams were sold.

Mannequins in straw hats surround us,
Strung up on birch crucifixes.
They are unbothered by the quivering
Internal jelly, the rushing of inner fluids
Or that green electric forest
Inside our brains we call a soul,
The place where dreams come from.
Their stale plastic heads are full of nothing at all

Yet their immaculate limbs will outlast
Every contract and leasehold,
Our imponderable good intentions
And the soft weight we use to enfold

Friends and family with warmth and love.
The dreamless among us feel no pain.
(But never will they plunge, head first, into the sea
And pull from the depths a nacre flame.)

I listen as Alice and Jack talk about
The delirious lullabies and sleepless nights
When primitive waves would crash
Against their heavy, hooded eyes
Returning varicoloured memories.
I may no longer understand their meanings,
Alice says, but dreams never disappear.
They live in us, like rings inside trees.

The sunset looks as though a god stubbed out
A limp cigar on its linen smock.
One of the kids makes xylophone music
On Jack's ribs; the other plucks
A toy stegosaurus from the dino pit
And furiously hurls it at the horizon.
Its kite-shaped spikes tear the astral fabric.
Light from an earlier place waters the garden.

III

Incantation to the Stone God

I fed wild strawberries into the mouth of the rock face
I watched the wild water rush over them and wash
The red from their flesh and the white from my flesh
I watched the wild red light fork across my palms
The white strawberries like quartz in the rushing water
I felt the red colour crash through my skin-barrier
And wild breath like ice fog eruct from the mouth
Of the stone god in the rock face on a cliff path
In my hands I held the mineral berries heavy as stars
In my mouth my heart sweet and full of red light
Anchored by a green chain, buttoned with bitter seeds
Bursting open, spilling beads of red heat down my chin
And the stone mouth of the stone god streamed with light
And swallowed the fruit I had so carelessly offered to it.

Crystal Lamp Auguries

Dark shadows from the windowpane
Fall over your bedspread like crosshairs.
There's nothing to hide. Nowhere.
I've been working all day in the sun.
My pockets are full of cherry stones,
Petals and chalk. They've overspilled,
And dirtied your floorboards.
I undress with the elegant atonality
Of a knife dropped on piano strings,
Then hold, courageously, for applause.

The legend of my masculinity precedes me.
It will disappoint us both. I'm a governor
Of inexpressible needs: beneath
My impulse to curate, and desire to win,
I want you to take complete control.
I will forfeit my language, burn
All my ambitions, and crawl to your feet
If you will only hurt me, again and again,
Then bundle me up in your shoebox
Like a sparrow with a broken wing.

*

Hard rock under the greasy moon.
I touched your arm.
Bruises, little bruises, like blue roses.
Wait until this part. It's the best part.
A tremolo like an angel.
A dripping wheel in the night.
(The outro is a button come undone.)
And those silhouettes, there,
What do they look like to you?
Men in trench coats; pines?
Or the shadows of others
You and I have touched.
Pulsating. Encircling us.

*

What was the promise you made to me
When we lay on your bed of straw?
The ringlets in our hair thatched together
On a clear dark night in December.
The world, you said, is like a water wheel
Turning all our misfortunes and fantasies
Up from pondweed into the light,
A rotation that goes on for ever, and ever . . .

What was the promise I made to you
When we lay on your bed of straw?
The lines on our palms pressed together
On a clear dark night in December.
Nothing, I said, has the power to undo us,
Not the moon snarling in the West
. Throwing silk against the wall,
Nor the strange pack of dogs in the snow.

*

Treasure, I think, *where are we going?*
Where do we go?

After a Dream by the Banks of the River Frome

I lie quiet as a newt in the knee-high grass
In shade cast by a caravan named Adria.
Dozens of swimmers dot the lawn
Suckling on lidos, or vaporisers,
Liberating phantasms from their throats
Which hang in the still air,
Commingling with barbecue smoke
Drifting through the trees. Like the bow
Of a fleshy ship emerging from mist
Appears the stomach of Chris Lilly,
Infamous house-flipper-cum-philanderer.
He covers the span of the hazy green
Carrying his infant son above his head
Who flaps like a sprite, in Batman armbands.

Lilly's torso is veneered with ink:
Three decades of spontaneous tattoos.
A mare and bustard in black silhouette,
Illuminated initials of exes, in vines,
And an ionic column stamped on his chest –
A pedestal for his heart, that his love
Might aspire to and finally rest
In the higher orders, and become
Unimpeachable, even after his flesh
Goes the way of all flesh: motes
And particulates in the knee-high grass
Clumped on stems and stamens;
Proteins in fox fur; tree sap in tree veins;
And eyes in plumes of peacock feathers.

Lilly builds up speed, approaching the bank.
The old muscles of his adolescence
Come out of retirement, and stretch
His tattoos into nonsense symbols,
Shocking the column with wrinkles.
By instinct, he estimates trajectories,
Imagining an ancient athlete
Hurling a javelin, or a marine
Lighting a cannon in the rain, in a war
For the bloody peace of England.
He launches his son into the air.
The boy seems to swim, or float up there,
His Day-Glo yellow bands buoying him
Aloft and haloed like two miniature suns.

*

The swimmers are tanned and iridescent,
Caked in sun-dried river syrup,
The water streaked with rainbows:
Gasoline seepage from Farmer Vagg's
Lime-green hillock, across the bank,
Hired out for the annual motocross tourney.
Hundreds of shimmering recreational vehicles
Are encrusted on the crest of the hill
Like metallic scales on a mythic beast.
A touch of ozone in the air. Frying meat.
The clerk of the course announces the racers:
Team GB versus Team USA, the latter
Captained by Cody 'The Knife' Garcia,
Legendary Californian famed for slashing records.

Gunfire. Engines. A chorus of chainsaws.
In the refreshments marquee, Farmer Vagg,
Straw-hatted, catnaps atop his antique
Walking-stick seat. He dreams his crops
Are swarmed with insects, exoskeletons
Glowing like fire. He dreams of his children,
Lost somewhere in the crystal spires,
Academies and office blocks of London
Like figurines inside an Escher drawing.
Vagg doesn't stir, even as the siren blares
And the clerk, over loudspeakers, declares
A driver down on track number one.
Cody The Knife has spilled his bike
And parts of him have been rearranged.

A bouquet has bloomed inside his helmet:
Blood, golden dirt and bad haze,
Pink foam issuing from his nose.
Through the cracked visor, Cody sees
A doorway mirrored with infinities
Opening out into the August sky,
Where summer lightning evanesces like imagination.
Cody perches atop a cloud of ice
And spies, on one side of the river,
A burning city full of burning men
Spitting Catherine Wheels of fire;
And on the other, a fertile country
Of sprawling plains and towering trees
That reminds him of America.

*

Lilly's boy floats on his back downstream
Bewitched by an air-ambulance helicopter,
Helix like a seed from a sycamore.
While he watches, Ms Dellar watches him,
Wondering if the boy will be the first
After three generations of slippery men
To live up to his name. Lilly, from *lilium*,
Figurative of light, fairness and innocence.
Ms Dellar, horticulturalist and historian,
Stands by the bank, shaking off emeralds.
Behind, her daughter's daughter, Elise,
Stretches her arms out wide, so that it seems
Dellar is a four-armed deity, whose body
Has endured over a century on this earth.

Elise is back from a study year in France,
Beleaguered by a summer romance.
A Parisian academic has stolen her heart,
And filled her head with troubling ideas.
England is dying, she says. England
Is already dead. Skin splits on her lips,
As though another woman's mouth
Were bursting through. In Dellar's eyes,
A man who doesn't see that there awaits,
In rot, the sticky machinery that yields
New beginnings, isn't much of a philosopher.
But she holds her peace, believing Elise
Must be threshed by desire's latticework
In order to learn its rare and exquisite pain.

The women lie down on a hand-sewn quilt
In thundercloud cover, and begin to sleep.
Dellar, from *dell-dweller*. What's in a name?
In her mind she plays a memory game,
Tracing the branches of her family tree,
The sugar planters, traders, politicians and thieves
Whose heredity dripped like blood through leaves
And converted indignation into wealth.
A honey-stone estate in the bowl of the valley
Where Dellar observes the lives of the county,
Propagating prescience. She goes observed
By none, but the dreamer, who wakes at last:
In shade cast by a caravan named Adria
I lie quiet as a newt in the knee-high grass.

With My Mother at the Cattle Market Car Boot

I wonder what it is you think is missing
From your life, that might be found here
In the misty rain, beside deserted cattle pens,
These rows on rows of slant trestle tables

Stacked with dog-eared books, mildewed lampshades:
Bric-a-brac poached from the clearances
Of dead people's houses, all across the watershed,
From Hemlock Wood to Horseshoe Bend.

It seems to me a gallery of future hauntings.
The longer we stay, I'm sure, the more likely it is
That we'll catch cold, or depression. Like you,
I still suspect that pain, and grief, are pathogens.

Here are black-and-white photographs
Of expressionless strangers, from the nineteen-forties
Held in a moth-eaten, leather-bound album,
Priced at a fiver. The relic of light in their faces

Causes my own to contort. I can't fathom
How this miraculous overabundance
Of life, and time, sealed by silver impressions
Has turned so casually into flotsam

Sold at a car boot by a drowsy ox of a man
Whose pipe-smoking uninterest in the origins
Of these photos seems to endorse nihilism.
Might be they came from a house in Frome.

Later, you buy a pair of concrete grotesques
Each twice the size of a human head
With anguished mouths, and eyes that solicit pity.
They will be placed on the pillar in your driveway.

One to ward off evil spirits – or those
Who would approach with ill intent –
The other as an invitation. Sit down child. Rest.
Here, even the tragic will find sanctuary.

On Visiting My Father's Grave

I didn't once visit, for years after the fact,
For fear that I would get stuck
In a place that had become mythical
In my imagination; that this would amount

To a metaphysical death, a departure from reality
That might prove irreversible.
When, on impulse, I at last ventured
Back into the valley known as Slaughterford,

I expected to find the spot erased; cordoned off,
Deluged with sewage, or built upon.
Part of me wanted this. It would seem to justify
The intolerable rage I carry within myself,

A rage that I refuse to attach to its proper place,
Which is that you – he – left, so soon,
Without ever giving me the chance
To interrogate him, as an adult; to ask advice

On fixing leaks, punctures, heartbreak,
Or when it's better to admit defeat;
To ask how I might help exorcise his demons,
That they not also inhabit me; and finally,

To ask why the world is how it is:
Cruel with redemptive kindnesses.
But he left. It was convenient. He could not
Disappoint with inadequate answers.

But to have witnessed his fallibility
Would have enabled us to encounter
One another as equals, and speak
The truth. But he – you – left. So soon.

The patch of marsh beneath the willow,
I found, was the same as ever.
The reeds reverberated with millions of insects,
And the millions of suns that power

Their musculature. It is tempting to believe
That some transmission was carried
On this static, that my father
Was trying to speak to me.

But what would he possibly want to say,
After so long? Perhaps only to ask
For a little understanding,
A little reassurance, just like the living.

Way Back West

I return to an old place. The road is red
And the sun gorges on itself.
The skyline is violet and dissolves into scorched hills.
The twilight, then, is undressed,
Revealing the violent cosiness of the stars.
Their silence feels odd, armed
With the knowledge that strange men spill
The guts of our talents wantonly
Into the black, for ever into distant spirals.
A barn, full of foxed mirrors.
Ghosts peek out from the edges,
Thirsting to remember how time went, once,
And the anecdotes and rivalries
That kept their bodies intact.
I slip away, through the slats
And approach the stone house.
Inside, there are stale crusts and mice.
A TV screen, caught in the cotton jaws
Of wood smoke, leaking from
The faulty wood stove.
A videotape is regurgitated again and again
Against the lagoon of white noise.
And I am astounded to find
That this old place is pleasant.
When it never used to be.
The fighting has stopped; the silence too.
The bales of hay are wet with dew.
And the backs of the sleeping cows in the field
Are like the great blue backs of whales in the sea.

Down in Hemlock Wood

for J & E

After the country, into more country.
The farmhouse is rented, and friends of friends
Lurk along a happy lane, with ends
Spin-drifting from carbon-tinted windows.
It's an impersonation of harvest:
Mud-spattered machines parked in a glade
In a wood by a ditch, and rotund
Blushed faces tumbling out, like baubles.

I was afraid to come, afraid to find
How much has changed (the sacks upon sacks
Of cut hair, long gone to the birds;
Deposits of exhausted strength made
In the domestic wilderness, for returns
Of blue eggs, and a brighter spirit, perhaps).
In different shades of wool we upend sticks
For bonfires, and the mothers, on toasting

Capfuls and thimblefuls of purpled gin,
Surrender, then stub out their secrets
(*How readily were the tranqs despatched*
And how hurriedly we gobbled them up
When you were young, much younger than today).
Someone's six-foot step-siblings – twins – emerge
From behind the trunk of a Corsican pine,
Toeing needles ever so quietly, in sequins.

If we down collars, and huff each other's necks,
Will we discover what kind of dirt
We've all been living in? A little test, to ensure
Nobody's formed an expensive habit
Of scrubbing themselves too clean. The twins
Move off into the farm's darker cloisters
(A canvas tent lashed with candlelight).
Cider is unloosed in back of the barn –

A grubby kind of gold, spent liberally
On questions: have we at last learned to shave
Without breaking out in spots? Or eyeing
The elongated dash of the blade's edge,
Wise to the embellishment dashes bring?
And what about those three a.m. terrors –
No, not tamed, yet. They always babble up
From anticipation, not the fact, of loss.

Especially in the midst of the best,
Painless moments: laughing all night long
In that famous district of lowing cows.
Perhaps you'll understand, it's been hard
For me to speak – to make sounds, I mean.
The truth is, I didn't want you all to know
How I've been living. Because I chose it,
And so it's mine to own, and account for.

But it's getting better, in this company,
Our cuffs dipped carelessly in ash and butter.
I watch you, storying the recent past
Around a lighter flame – blue, orange, blue –

And my heart flutters, then swells, for my boys.
My boys, who are my girls, and vice versa.
They still love one another with ease
And without profit. I find that difficult

To imagine, if I'm honest, these days.
But the proof's in the patient exchanging
Of strings: letting fingers bleed on bronze
In a ring in the grass by the fire,
As white flowers, wrapped around stems,
Disassociate apples from their branches
Which fall into the deep, starry pond.
After all, it is the last night of summer

And you can't have a good country party
Without rewriting a few country songs.
If you're honey, I'm honey, honey.
If you're lonely and lost, I am too.
Flames lick the dark and crack like spines.
It's time to shake off the old avatar.
Some, for instance, mash pills to a caulk
With their molars, or take turns to sniff

The tip of a key to a haunted house.
Others only wish to fit their dozy heads
Into the crooks of shoulders, and drool.
One forgets how comfy the ground is,
With *just enough* give, like the relief
Of surrendering bad faith to the good
In good time, and without spite, or rancour.
The twins can be glimpsed in silhouette

Dashing across the dew. They light their way
By a candelabra scabbed in wax,
And track their trolleyed mother to the base
Of an ancient sycamore, where she loafs.
They brush broken glass from her blistered feet
To honour the oath, the sycamore tax:
Some of us must always be hunched over,
Sweeping, for the contentment of the rest.

Incantation to the Stone God

I prayed. I prayed and prayed.
I prayed until I ran out of language.
Then I prayed in colours.
I prayed in waves of white panic.

Each wave took something from me.
Each wave brought something back.
Small embers from elsewhere;
That pale ocean. Common prayer.

A wave came and took away my name.
A wave came and returned a stone.
The stone was smooth, flat and green.
I lodged it under my tongue.

I prayed again. I prayed and prayed
Until the stone began to draw
All the static and all the noise
That carousels inside my brain.

And when at last the noise was gone
I spat the stone into my hand.
I breathed, and felt as light and happy
As I had felt when I was a child.

Epigraph: from 'Are You Leaving for the Country' (Richard Tucker), performed by Karen Dalton, *In My Own Time* (1971).

The Poet's Dream: This poem uses and repurposes lines from *The Memoirs of John Addington Symonds*, a poet, historian and early sexual theorist, who lived in Bristol. Symonds was convinced by a friend to lock many of his poems away, and dispose of the key in a river.

Operation Galileo: This is the name of a national police operation which putatively aims to tackle hare coursing and poaching, and to protect the private property said to be damaged by such activities. This police operation has no remit for or interest in tackling other forms of illegal bloodsport, such as fox hunting. Some argue it is a Trojan horse operation, used to monitor and intimidate members of the Gypsy, Roma and Travelling communities. The epigraph is from Aesop's fable 'The Hares and the Frogs'.

Wych Elm Fields: This poem takes as its narrative inspiration the fate of two permanent, council-owned Gypsy, Roma and Traveller sites in the West Country. These sites were neglected by the county council for many years, despite the protestations of the residents, resulting in conditions that were unfit to live in (including, but not limited to, unsafe electrics, damp, lack of heating, pests, structural disrepair). Funding provided by the government to issue improvements to these sites was not effectively utilised, and subsequently rescinded. The council then sold these sites to private buyers. The residents had no say in the matter.

Hunter's Farm: A British huntsman and farmer, who was authorised to collect and dispose of fallen stock, was charged with breaching biosecurity measures: feeding contaminated specified risk material (SRM) to hounds and chickens; mixing SRM with other animal by-products; leaving animal carcasses to rot outside of specified bins, thereby enabling wildlife to feed on them. He was handed a twelve-month community order and ordered to pay a small fine. In 2022, the same man was secretly filmed shooting ten healthy hounds within the space of forty minutes. He was subsequently heard to remark, 'I love them [. . .] these are my life'.

ACKNOWLEDGEMENTS

I wish to thank my agent, Seren Adams, and my editors at Penguin, for their encouragement and belief in this work. I am extremely grateful to the Jan Michalski Foundation for providing a residency where the idea for this book first took shape, and to the Hawthornden Foundation for providing a residency where I continued to write it. Grateful acknowledgement is made to the editors of the following publications, where some of these poems (or earlier versions of them) first appeared: *Fantastic Man*, *Hotel* and *Tenement*, *The Center for Archaic Networks*, *The Poetry Review*, and *The Stinging Fly*. Thank you to the local librarians, artists, archivists and activists, from whom I take inspiration. Thank you, as always, to my loved ones.